Robert and the Instant Millionaire Show

by Barbara Seuling
Illustrated by Paul Brewer

A
LITTLE APPLE
PAPERBACK

SCHOLASTIC INC.
New York Toronto London Auckland Sydney
Mexico City New Delhi Hong Kong Buenos Aires

To Caleb Mansfield, who shared his story
—B. S.

To Tony Jacobson, Laura Tillotson,
and John Grandits
—P. B.

ISBN 0-439-35376-9

12 11 10 9 8 7 6 5 4 3 2 1   4 5 6 7 8 9/0

Printed in the U.S.A.

Contents

A Million Dollars

"Listen to this," said Robert, reading from his notebook. "Some lizards are born with no eyes." He took a sip of orange juice as he waited for a response.

"Get out of here," said Charlie, slurping the last mouthful of cereal from his bowl. "Nothing is born with no eyes."

"Stop slurping," said their mother. "Eat slowly. It's better for your digestion."

"It's true," said Robert. "It's in *Weird & Wacky Facts #33*. Here's another one: Earthworms grow to eleven feet long in Australia."

Charlie sprang up from his seat and grabbed his book bag. "Gotta go. Hockey practice today. I'll be home late."

Before anyone could say anything, Charlie was out the door and gone. Robert read his mom one more fact before he got up.

"Mom, listen. People used to think a runny nose meant your brain was leaking."

His mom smiled and put her coffee cup down. "Very interesting, Robert, but save the book for later. Paul is waiting on his corner for you."

Robert put the book of facts in his book bag and hurried out the door. He and his best friend, Paul, were trying to see how smart they could get by memorizing all the facts their heads could hold. Then they could get on *The Instant Millionaire* show and make a million dollars.

A couple of weeks ago, he and Paul had mailed in a postcard to *The Instant Million-aire*, asking to be contestants. They used an old postcard Robert had found in the stationery drawer. It had a picture of Niagara Falls on the front.

"What would you do with a million dollars?" Paul had asked him then.

"I'd get a computer. I have to use my mom's now. I'd buy a gazillion packs of gummy bears and . . . an electric guitar."

"An electric guitar?" said Paul. "You don't play the guitar."

"Oh. Well, I can take lessons, if I have a million dollars," said Robert. "What about you? What would you get?"

"Me? Oh, lots of paints and brushes like a real artist. And maybe a mountain bike. I like that new electronic game, *Asteroid Attack,* but if I get it, Nick would probably destroy it." Nick was Paul's little brother, who got into Paul's things sometimes.

It was fun planning what they would do with a million dollars. They would share it because they were going to be each

other's "Instant Buddy." You were allowed to have an Instant Buddy—someone to help you with your answers. They would be each other's Instant Buddy, because they were best friends, and because they were both going to memorize all the *Weird & Wacky Facts*.

Weird & Wacky Facts

"**G**ood morning, class," said Mrs. Bernthal as the children filed into the room. A new word was written in big letters on the chalkboard. Mrs. Bernthal gave them a new word to practice every day. They had to use the word three times during the day in conversation. Today's word was *ambitious*.

"I'm ambitious to become a famous artist," said Paul.

"I'm ambitious to read all the facts in the *Weird & Wacky Facts* series and memorize them," said Robert. Ever since he had met writer Frank Farraday during an author visit to his class, Robert wanted to know about everything. That's the kind of contestant they liked on *The Instant Millionaire.*

"I answered questions up to the $500 level last week," he told Paul at lunchtime.

Paul was impressed. "I only got up to $250," he said.

"We have to be ambitious and reach a higher level this week," said Robert.

Paul nodded. "Yeah."

The amount of money increased with each new level. The questions got harder and harder. Robert couldn't wait for next week's show. That was the hardest part of all. Waiting. The good part was that he had time to memorize a lot more facts. He was going to read and memorize all the books in the *Weird & Wacky Facts* series. He had almost all of them. The only ones missing were #11 and #23.

Lester Willis sat down at their lunch table.

"Hi, Lester," said Robert, taking out his *Weird & Wacky Facts #33.*

"Hi, guys," said Lester. "What are you doing?"

"Memorizing facts," said Robert, "so we can get really smart."

"Cool," said Lester. "I have one of those books."

"Bring it in and practice memorizing facts with us," said Robert. "It's fun."

"Okay," said Lester. He took his sandwich out of a brown paper bag and bit into it.

Later that afternoon, Mrs. Bernthal put a box on her desk. It was the familiar box that their book club books always came in. Robert and Paul had both ordered the latest *Weird & Wacky Facts* book, #34.

"You are going to be the smartest boys in the school," Mrs. Bernthal said with a smile.

Susanne Lee Rodgers got three books. Two were stories that had won some kind of medal. The third was a book about Amelia Earhart, a pilot. Susanne looked at the books in Robert's and Paul's hands.

"You should read some good books sometime," she said, looking at the boys as though they were bugs. Robert couldn't help grinding his teeth when Susanne Lee looked at him like that.

"This is a good book," said Paul. "It's excellent."

Susanne Lee just walked back to her table, her hair bouncing.

"What's her problem?" said Robert.

"Maybe she thinks we will become smarter than she is."

Robert thought of what Mrs. Bernthal had said. "Hey, Paul," he said. "Do you think that's possible?"

"What?" said Paul.

"That we could be as smart as—or smarter than—Susanne Lee?"

"I don't know," said Paul.

Robert wondered how Susanne Lee got so smart. She didn't even read *Weird & Wacky Facts*.

Class Project

"**I**'d like your attention, class," said Mrs. Bernthal when they settled in the next morning. There were pictures of famous bridges tacked up on the bulletin board. Robert recognized the Brooklyn Bridge. His family drove over that bridge when they visited Coney Island and the aquarium.

"What does a bridge do?" Mrs. Bernthal asked. That seemed pretty easy.

"It crosses a river," Lester Willis called out. Lester always called out. No matter how many times Mrs. Bernthal told him to

raise his hand, he still shouted out whatever he had to say.

Mrs. Bernthal called on Susanne Lee,
who always raised her hand. "A bridge lets
you cross from one place to another," said
Susanne Lee.

"Right," said Mrs. Bernthal.

Mrs. Bernthal talked about all kinds of
bridges, even the bridge of your nose and
the bridge on a violin. She said some people
had artificial teeth called bridges, because
they crossed from one tooth to another.

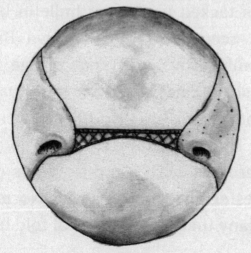

"We're going to learn about the kind of bridges that people build to walk or ride across," Mrs. Bernthal said. "I want you to choose a study partner for the next two weeks."

At their table, Robert and Paul did a high five. They knew they would be partners.

"You may study any bridge you like," said Mrs. Bernthal. "Do a report on it. Explain what kind of bridge it is and how it is made. Make a model of it and tell us why you chose that bridge."

"What bridge do you want to do?" Paul asked Robert.

"I don't know," said Robert. "Let's find one that's really unusual."

"Unusual how?" asked Paul.

"I don't know," Robert said, scratching his head. "I want ours to be different."

"Come over to my house after school tomorrow," said Paul. "We'll check out bridges on the Internet." Paul always had good ideas. He also had his own computer.

"Did you know that the kiwi bird has no wings?" said Robert at dinner that night.

Mr. Dorfman's eyebrows went up as he chewed on a chicken wing, but he didn't say a word.

"That's a pretty useless bird, then," said Charlie. "It might as well be a cat."

"Have some broccoli, Robert," said Mrs. Dorfman.

Robert put a piece of broccoli on his plate. "In some places, people use feathers for money." He took a bite of his drumstick.

"I'd like to go to a place like that," said Robert's mom. "First I would collect all the duck feathers in Van Saun Park."

"How was practice today?" Robert's dad asked Charlie.

"Great," said Charlie, wolfing down a
piece of corn bread. "I made two goals.
Coach said he wants me to do some work
with weights to strengthen my legs."

"What's wrong with your legs?" asked
Mrs. Dorfman.

"Nothing," said Charlie. "It's just what hockey players do so they can skate faster and better. I think Coach might make me captain next year."

Robert's dad looked pleased. "That's terrific," he said. He turned to Robert. "And how's the Instant Millionaire?"

"Fine. I'm almost finished memorizing book #33."

Robert was glad his father had asked. Memorizing facts was hard work, after doing homework, and working on projects, and feeding Fuzzy, his pet tarantula, and his two doves, Flo and Billie. His head hurt sometimes from so much remembering.

Galloping Gertie

Robert and Paul had been working on their bridge report for an hour already. Paul sat at his computer, clicking away. Pages and pages on all kinds of bridges were taped to the walls. More papers were on the bed. There was the history of bridges. There were famous bridges. There were pictures of the oldest bridge, the longest bridge, the bridge that had the most traffic. And they still hadn't decided which bridge they would work on.

Robert got up to stretch. He wandered over to the bookshelf and picked up a dark blue cardboard folder. The folder opened like a book and showed each state and its new quarter plus state birds, mottoes, and flowers. New Jersey's state flower was the violet. The state bird was the goldfinch. The motto was "Liberty and Prosperity." Robert noticed that the cardinal appeared as the state bird for several states. He put the quarter collection back on the shelf.

"We can do London Bridge," said Robert, going back to the pages on Paul's bed. "The one that was in the old nursery rhyme. Remember? 'London Bridge is falling down, falling down, falling down. . . .'"

"We could, but it doesn't say anything about it really falling down. Now, *that* would be interesting," said Paul.

"It's time to relinquish your seat," said

Robert, using Mrs. Bernthal's latest word.
"Let me try it."

Robert followed one link after another.
"Look!" He found a pontoon bridge. "This

bridge floats on the water," he said. Paul agreed that it had possibilities. Robert printed out that page.

He went back to surf some more. He found a bridge in Tacoma, Washington, that had twisted and turned so badly when the wind blew that it tore itself in two. There were pictures of it right on the computer screen. You could get seasick just from looking at them.

"Paul. Take a look. This is great."

Paul hooted when he saw it. "They called it Galloping Gertie!" he said.

"Let's do this one," said Robert.

Paul agreed. They had their bridge. It was not only a bridge. It was a bridge disaster! Cool.

Leonardo da Vinky

On Saturday, Paul came over on his bike to work on the model of Galloping Gertie. Robert's mom went off to the flea market, as she did every Saturday morning.

"I'll be back in time to fix you boys lunch," she called to them. "If you need a snack, there are some apple muffins in the fridge. And juice drinks."

"Okay, Mom," said Robert. He wished the muffins were homemade, like at Paul's house, but at least there was something to eat if they got hungry.

They spent the morning constructing a bridge that looked like the one in the pictures. Twice it collapsed, and they had to start all over again. They used all kinds of building materials. It was Paul's idea to use spaghetti boxes for the two towers that held the cables. Robert put the spaghetti into a plastic bag so they could use the boxes.

Paul found some rope they could use for the cables. With plenty of glue and tape, they held the pieces together. They connected old toy train tracks and used them for the roadway that carried cars across. By the time Robert's mom got home and made lunch, their version of Galloping Gertie was beginning to look pretty good.

They had melted cheese sandwiches for lunch. Robert's mom sat down with them and ate one, too.

"So how are you doing with your project?" she asked.

"Which one?" asked Paul.

"Oh. Didn't you say you had to build a bridge?"

"Yes," said Paul. "But I thought maybe you were asking about *The Instant Millionaire*. The bridge is okay so far."

"Well, how is the Instant Millionaire project going, then?"

"Great!" said Robert, before Paul could answer. "You want to hear some more facts?"

"Sure," said Mrs. Dorfman.

"You go first, Paul," said Robert.

Paul started. "Even if there are 80,000 bees in one hive, only one of them, the queen, can be a mother." He looked at Robert, signaling for him to go next.

"A famous artist named Leonardo da Vinky wrote all his notes backward so nobody could read them," Robert said.

Mrs. Dorfman smiled. "Very good," she said, "but it's da Vinci, Robert, with a *ch* sound, not a *k*."

"Oh. Thanks." Robert was pleased that his mom was listening to them. "Did you like those facts?"

"Yes, I liked them very much."

Robert walked Paul to the door.

"We've got to get up to $1,000 this week," said Paul.

"Let's memorize ten new facts by tomorrow," said Robert.

"Okay," said Paul. "Do you think memorizing facts really makes us smarter?"

"I don't know," said Robert, "but Mrs. Bernthal said so."

The $125,000 Question

Aunt Julie and Uncle Dan came for dinner on Sunday. At first, Robert thought he would be trapped for the day listening to dull grown-up talk. Or worse, sports talk, if Charlie had anything to do with it. But he was surprised.

"What's this?" asked Uncle Dan, reaching from the big overstuffed chair to the coffee table. He picked up one of Robert's *Weird & Wacky Facts* books.

"Oh, nothing," said Robert. "Just a book of facts."

"I used to love these when I was a kid," said Uncle Dan. *"Ripley's Believe It or Not* was in the Sunday papers, and there were whole books of Ripley's facts, too."

"Robert seems to be obsessed with odd facts," said Mr. Dorfman, winking at Robert.

Robert was not sure "obsessed" was a good thing to be, since he didn't know what the word meant, but it couldn't be too bad, since his dad winked.

"Well, I think a boy's got a right to have a passion for some things," said Uncle Dan. "I had baseball cards and comic books and G.I. Joe. They were all pretty important to me. And I didn't turn out so badly." He laughed. Robert's dad laughed, too.

"I guess that's true enough," he said.

After dinner, the women started telling family stories. Robert loved this part of their visits, especially when his mom and Aunt Julie talked about when they were kids. They mentioned things Robert had never heard of—pet rocks, mood rings, and tie-dyeing (whatever that was).

Before they knew it, it was seven-thirty.

"Look at the time, Dan," said Aunt Julie. "We have an hour's drive to Connecticut. We'd better get going."

"Why don't you stay and watch *The Instant Millionaire* with us?" asked Robert's mom. "Robert insists we see it. You won't get home in time to watch it yourselves. I'll put on another pot of coffee."

They agreed and settled into the living room. The smell of brewing coffee soon filled the house. Robert loved that smell. He had tasted coffee once, but it didn't taste as good as it smelled.

The music played, and the lights flashed blue and green and purple. In a little spot in the center of the screen was Todd Edwards, the host.

"Welcome to another show, ladies and gentlemen, where ordinary people like YOU"—he pointed right at the camera—"can become instant millionaires!"

Tonight a woman got up to the $50,000 level. The suspense built as she answered the question: What do you call the implement that you use to turn over hamburgers? Is it a ladle, a tureen, a spatula, or a whisk?

"A spatula?"

The woman got it right. Robert made a

mental note to add the word *spatula* to his word list. He liked the way it sounded.

By the time the coffee was ready, the woman had won $75,000, then $100,000. She was ready for the $125,000 question. Robert's parents and his aunt and uncle were just as excited as he was now. You could feel the tension when Todd Edwards asked, "Which bird is represented more than any other as a state bird?"

Robert gulped. He knew the answer. He had seen it in Paul's quarter collection. "The cardinal," he said. The clock ticked. The woman was sweating. She didn't know the answer. She had used up her three Instant Buddy turns. The buzzer went off.

"Oh, I'm sorry," said Todd Edwards. "It's the cardinal."

Everyone turned to Robert.

"Robert! How did you know that?" said Aunt Julie.

Robert shrugged and smiled politely. His mom and dad looked at him as if they weren't sure who he was.

"Yo, bro," said Charlie. "Not bad."

Wow. Even Charlie was impressed.

Aunt Julie and Uncle Dan left after the program was over. Robert went upstairs to call Paul. Wait until he told him he'd answered the $125,000 question!

The Phone Call

Getting the bridge to school was the hardest part. The model was glued to a large piece of cardboard. Robert carried it down the stairs from his room, slowly and carefully. He set it on the floor by the door while he slurped down a glass of juice and gobbled a toaster tart.

"Take your time, Rob," said his mom. Robert wiped the crumbs off his mouth and wiggled into his backpack straps. As he picked up the bridge model, his mom got up to open the door. "Just walk slowly," she said. "And good luck."

"Thanks," said Robert, balancing the board in front of him.

The bridge swayed as badly as the original Galloping Gertie had done. By the time Robert got to Paul's corner, his arms hurt from trying to keep the board straight.

"We both have to carry it," he said. "I don't think I can make it to school without having all our work collapse." Paul agreed and held up one side of the board. Since he was quite a bit taller than Robert, the board was on a slant.

"Why don't we use Nick's wagon?" asked Paul.

"Good idea," said Robert. They were close enough to Paul's house to get the wagon and still be in time for school.

Paul's mom came to the door. "What happened? Why aren't you in school?"

"Hi, Mrs. Felcher," said Robert. "We're having trouble carrying our bridge."

"Can we borrow Nick's wagon?" asked Paul.

"Sure, I guess so," said Paul's mom.

They laid the board down on the front step while Paul went into the garage to get the wagon. Meanwhile, Nick toddled up to his mom to see what was going on. Paul came out with the wagon. In it was a small portable fan.

"I thought we could use this," said Paul.

Robert put the model next to the fan. Nick ran over and tried to climb into the wagon.

"No, no, Nick," said Paul. "You can't go this time."

Nick howled. Mrs. Felcher picked him up, but he only screamed louder.

"Hey, Nick," said Robert, trying to calm him down, "we'll bring it back."

"Let's just go. Fast." Paul raced down the driveway with the wagon bouncing along behind him.

"Slow down," said Robert, about a block from Paul's house. "We don't want a bridge disaster until later."

Matt Blakey and Joey Rizzo did their report first, on the George Washington Bridge in New York City. Matt passed out photographs of the bridge that he had taken himself. The construction was made out of coat hangers, cardboard, and string. Joey rolled a tiny car over the bridge. Other toy cars and trucks were glued to the roadway.

Emily Asher and Kristi Mills showed something that looked like a house. Kristi talked about covered bridges while Emily walked around the room with their model.

"The roof kept the bridge clear of snow and ice," Kristi said. "That made it easier for horses to get across."

When it was their turn, Robert and Paul wheeled their bridge to the front of the classroom. They lifted it out of the wagon onto a table. Paul talked about suspension bridges and how they were built. Robert explained what had happened after the Tacoma bridge was completed.

"The wind made the bridge sway," he said. Paul turned on the fan to LOW. The rope cables on their bridge moved a little.

"The wind got stronger," said Robert, "and the bridge began to sway to and fro." Paul turned up the fan to MEDIUM. Nothing happened.

"It's a good thing cars stopped going across . . ." said Robert, giving Paul a sign. Paul turned the fan up to HIGH. ". . . because

there was a windstorm. Before long the bridge twisted itself in two and collapsed." The model blew over on its side.

Robert looked down at the bridge. "It really didn't fall over like this one did," he added. "It twisted like a crazy roller coaster. That's when they nicknamed the bridge 'Galloping Gertie.' It finally collapsed, and that was the end of it."

The class applauded. Robert and Paul took bows.

The rest of the morning went quickly as they watched and listened to the other bridge reports.

Robert was really hungry at lunchtime. He was about to take a bite of his sandwich when Lester bounced up.

"Hey, Rob," he said, plunking down across from Robert. "What's in your sandwich?"

"Baloney and cheese."

"What's in yours?" Lester asked Paul.

"Tuna fish."

"I got sardines," said Lester. Robert hated sardines. He even hated the smell of them. Lester opened his sandwich, and Robert tried not to make a face.

Lester took out a *Weird & Wacky Facts* book. The cover was ripped and the pages were worn, but Robert saw that it was #11—one of the two that he didn't have in his collection.

"Lester, where did you get that?" asked Robert.

"This? I don't know," said Lester. "It's been around the house for a long time."

"Don't you remember?"

Lester shrugged. "No. You want it?"

Robert gasped. "Really? You'd give me your book?"

"Sure. Maybe in return for your sandwich." Lester stared at Robert's baloney and cheese.

Robert looked down at his sandwich. He pushed it toward Lester.

"For a whole week," added Lester.

"It's a deal," Robert said.

Lester handed the book to Robert. "You can have this, too," said Lester, pushing his sardine sandwich across the table.

"Thanks," said Robert, not wanting to hurt Lester's feelings.

The minute the bell rang and Lester looked the other way, Robert tossed the sandwich in the trash.

When they got to Robert's house after school, Robert was starving. He grabbed a bag of chips and had just ripped them open when his mom walked in.

"Hi, boys," she said. "You got a phone call, Rob. From *The Instant Millionaire*."

Robert almost choked on a chip. "Mmrrot . . . mmffft . . . What . . . did they want?" He coughed to clear the chip from his throat.

"Well, when they asked for you, I said you were in school. When they found out how old you are, they said you could not be a contestant on the show. Contestants have to be over eighteen years old."

Robert's dream of fame and fortune came crashing down. Paul was pretty bummed out, too. They went up to Robert's room.

"Maybe we were too ambitious," said Robert, flopping down on the beanbag chair.

"Maybe we're not prominent enough," said Paul, using their new vocabulary word. He flopped down on the beanbag chair next to Robert. It was where they did their best thinking.

"Over eighteen!" said Robert.

Paul tossed up a chip and caught it in his mouth. "I didn't know you had to be old to get on the show," he said.

"By the time we're eighteen," said Robert, "there will probably be a gazillion more *Weird & Wacky Facts* books!"

Paul said, in a voice like a TV reporter, "Robert Dorfman and Paul Felcher, once members of Mrs. Bernthal's class, memorized every fact in the *Weird & Wacky Facts* series, except for books #23, #492, and #2,359."

Robert continued, "They were so ambitious that they went on to memorize the entire Encyclopaedia Britannica . . ."

"And the dictionary . . ." said Paul.

"And the *Guinness Book of World Records,* too . . ." Robert added.

"Before they relinquished their place in Mrs. Bernthal's class to become prominent world leaders," finished Paul.

Paul tossed another chip up in the air. They both went for it at the same time, mouths open. *BONK!*

"Ow!"

"Ouch!"

They rubbed their heads and looked at each other. Then they laughed so hard they rolled off the beanbag in a heap.

Over Eighteen

After Paul left, Robert thought again about *The Instant Millionaire.* Maybe they could find someone who was over eighteen who could go on the show for them. He or Paul could be that person's Instant Buddy, to help with the harder questions. But who would it be?

It had to be someone who knew a lot about everything. His dad knew a lot about math. Frank Farraday knew all there was to know about animals. But that wasn't enough. Robert needed someone who knew a lot about a gazillion different things.

At last he thought of the perfect person. Mrs. Bernthal! She knew everything. Robert thought about all the things Mrs. Bernthal knew. She knew lots of vocabulary words. She knew about Native Americans, Pilgrims, and presidents. She knew math and all the state capitals, and how to spell every word in the spelling book. She knew about rain forests, dinosaurs, plants, the flag, pollution, and more. She even knew about snakes. Mrs. Bernthal had bought them a beautiful green ribbon snake named Sally and taught them how to take care of her. And Mrs. Bernthal was over eighteen for sure.

Robert was so excited, he didn't even remember to call Paul first. He thumped downstairs to the den and opened the stationery drawer. He picked out another postcard from the bunch in the rubber band. This one was from the Luray Caverns in Virginia.

Next, he pulled out the telephone book and looked up Mrs. Bernthal's address and telephone number. He wrote on the left side of the postcard:

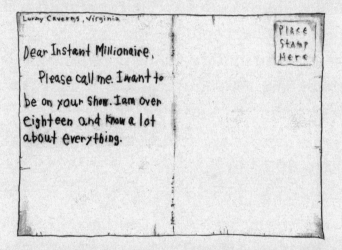

Luray Caverns, Virginia

Dear Instant Millionaire,

Please call me. I want to be on your show. I am over eighteen and know a lot about everything.

PLACE
STAMP
HERE

Underneath, he wrote Mrs. Bernthal's name, address, and telephone number. On the right side of the postcard, he wrote in the address of *The Instant Millionaire* show, just as he had before. He found a stamp in the drawer and stuck it on the corner of the postcard.

He went back upstairs and put the post-card in his book bag to mail on the way to school in the morning.

Oops!

Robert was starving. Again he had had to give up his lunch for a sardine sandwich. Didn't Lester ever bring anything else for lunch? He grabbed a slice of American cheese and a juice drink from the refrigerator and went upstairs to check on his animals.

The birds twittered as Robert entered his room. "Hi, Flo. Hi, Billie." It was nice to have the doves greet him, especially when no one else was home. He opened the cage door and let them fly around the room for their exercise.

The phone rang. Robert went to answer it on the upstairs landing.

"Dorfman residence, Robert speaking." Robert answered the phone just as he had been taught to do.

"This is Mike Cosmo of Cosmo's Collectibles," said a man's voice. "Is Mrs. Dorfman there?" Robert told him she was not and asked if he could take a message.

"Tell her I'm the guy she met at the flea market Saturday. I want to buy her postcard collection. She'll know what I'm talking about." Mr. Cosmo spelled his name for Robert. "Tell her I will be at the flea market this coming Saturday if she's interested."

Uh-oh. Those postcards he used—could they have been from his mom's collection? He thought they were just old, leftover cards.

After he hung up, Robert went to the den and found the postcards in the stationery

50

drawer again. He took off the rubber band and spread them out like a fan. The Grand Canyon. Miami Beach. Alaska. Mount Desert Island, Maine. The Badlands. Cheyenne, Wyoming. Salt Lake City, Utah. They were from all over the country.

He noticed this time that some of the cards had been written on, but they were to and from people Robert had never heard of.

When his mom came home, Robert gave her the message from Mr. Cosmo.

"That's great," she said. "I had a feeling those postcards were worth something."

With a funny feeling in his stomach, Robert asked, "What postcards was Mr. Cosmo talking about, Mom?"

"I've been saving old postcards for years," she told him. "I have quite a collection."

"The ones in the stationery drawer?"

"Yes. Plus a few shoe boxes full upstairs. I used to think I would travel to all the places on those postcards."

Robert gulped. It was getting harder to speak. "Did you?"

"No. I met your father, and he doesn't like to travel that much." Mrs. Dorfman sighed.

Robert tried to tell his mom about the two postcards he had used for *The Instant Millionaire,* but his voice wouldn't come out. What if they were worth a lot of money? Robert felt his stomach do a flip.

"I think we should have Chinese food tonight," said Robert's dad as he entered the room. "I'll go and pick it up. What does everyone want? The usual?"

"That's fine with me," said Robert's mom. "And you, Rob?" Robert shrugged. He wasn't very hungry, even for Chinese food.

"What's wrong, Rob?" asked his mom later, when the food came. He was poking the fried dumpling on his plate with his fork.

"Nothing," said Robert. He picked up the dumpling and nibbled around its edges. He put it back down.

"Are you sure?" said his mom. "You usually love fried dumplings."

"May I be excused?" Robert said.

His mom looked surprised. "Of course," she said. "Are you feeling all right?"

"Yes. I mean, no. I mean, yes. I'm just tired."

"Well, go on," said his mom. "If you get hungry later, we can heat up some leftovers for you."

Robert left the table and went up to his room. He lay on his bed and stared at the ceiling. How was he going to tell his mom what he had done? Maybe now Mr. Cosmo wouldn't want her postcard collection. Maybe his mom had lost out on a gazillion dollars because of what he'd done.

Robert rolled over on his stomach and wondered how many flea markets he'd have to walk through before he could replace his mom's postcards.

There was a knock on his door.

"Rob, I'm worried about you," said his mom, coming in. "Are you okay?"

Robert rolled over on his back again and sat up. "Mom, I used two of those postcards," he said.

"The postcards?" she repeated. "In the desk?"

Robert nodded.

"How come?" She didn't seem angry.

"I thought they were just old, leftover cards," said Robert. "I needed to write postcards to someone."

"Ah," said his mom. "Of course. They were right there in the stationery drawer." She smiled. "They wouldn't have been sent to *The Instant Millionaire* now, would they?"

"Yes," Robert said. "Were they worth a lot of money?"

"Well, not a *lot* of money. I don't think two cards will make much of a difference to Mr. Cosmo, if that's what's worrying you."

"Oh, that's good," said Robert. He felt better. "How come you saved all those cards for so long and now you want to sell them?"

"I don't need them anymore," she said.

"How come?"

"I decided to stop dreaming and start doing," his mom answered.

"Doing? You mean go someplace?" Robert felt a stab of loneliness just at the thought of his mom leaving. He had missed her terribly the last time she had to go on a trip for her job.

"Not me alone. All of us. Maybe we'll go skiing this winter."

Robert actually thought that could be fun. Skiing was not like hockey, or baseball, or other jock sports. Skiing couldn't be much different from playing in the snow with his sled.

"All I have to do is convince your dad," said his mother.

"Oh, yeah. That won't be easy, will it?" said Robert. He thought of how his dad hated trips and loved his recliner and his videotape collection, neatly arranged in alphabetical order on a shelf in the den.

"Oh, I don't know," said his mom. She had a twinkle in her eye. "I found out there's going to be a convention of math and science teachers in Aspen, Colorado, this winter. If we can lure your dad to that, we can ski all day while he goes to stuffy old meetings. He can join us on the slopes if he gets bored with math."

Maybe Robert had to stop dreaming and start doing, too. *The Instant Millionaire* was dreaming. He didn't need a million dollars. He and Paul had plenty of fun without an electric guitar and a mountain bike. He ran to the telephone to call Paul and tell him.

BARBARA SEULING is a well-known author of fiction and nonfiction books for children, including several books about Robert. She divides her time between New York City and Vermont.

PAUL BREWER likes to draw gross, silly situations, which is why he enjoys working on books about Robert so much. He lives in San Diego, California, with his wife and two daughters.

Also by Barbara Seuling

Oh No, It's Robert

Robert and the Attack of the Giant Tarantula

Robert and the Snake Escape

Robert and the Great Pepperoni

Robert and the Sneaker Snobs

Robert and the Instant Millionaire *Show*

Robert and the Three Wishes

3 WISHES

by Barbara Seuling
Illustrated by Paul Brewer

A
LITTLE APPLE
PAPERBACK

SCHOLASTIC INC.
New York   Toronto   London   Auckland   Sydney
Mexico City   New Delhi   Hong Kong   Buenos Aires

To my wonderful writers' group—Bonnie Bryant, Miriam Cohen, Sandra Jordan, Peter Lerangis, Ellen Levine, Fran Manushkin, Harry Mazer, Norma Fox Mazer, and Marvin Terban—for their support, love, and laughter
—B. S.

For Gary, Aline, and Cyrus
—P. B.

Contents

The Contest

Robert rolled his pencil back and forth as Mrs. Bernthal talked.

"Class, I received a very interesting letter," said Mrs. Bernthal, "from *The Instant Millionaire* show."

Robert stopped the pencil in mid-roll and looked at his best friend, Paul, who sat on the other side of the table. Paul looked back at him and shrugged.

"*The Instant Millionaire* show!" shouted Lester Willis. Lester Willis always called out without raising his hand.

1

"Yes," said Mrs. Bernthal. "*The Instant Millionaire* show."

"Wow!" said Emily Asher. Everyone turned to look at her. Emily Asher almost never called out. She probably couldn't help herself. *The Instant Millionaire* show was the most popular show on TV. People won a million dollars for answering questions correctly.

"I don't know how they got my name," Mrs. Bernthal said with a smile.

Robert wiggled in his seat. He had sent in a postcard to *The Instant Millionaire* show with Mrs. Bernthal's name on it. She was the smartest person he knew. He couldn't be a contestant himself because you had to be eighteen years old to be on the show. He had told Paul about sending the postcard. Paul looked like he was squirming in his seat, too.

"Unfortunately," continued Mrs. Bernthal, "I can't be a contestant on that show.

I have a cousin who works for the TV station, and there's a rule. Close relatives of employees cannot be on their game shows."

Robert relaxed. At least Mrs. Bernthal wasn't mad. "I like contests," she went on. "They are lots of fun, and they encourage you to think. Since you are the best class in the whole school, I'm going to let you have a contest of your own. It will be a week from Monday. That will give you time to prepare."

"Yeah!" shouted Joey Rizzo. "For a million dollars?"

"Oooooh!" squealed Melissa Thurm.

"Cool!" said Brian Hoberman.

"It will work just like the TV show, except for the money, of course," said Mrs. Bernthal. There were a few groans. "We'll use points instead. The boys will be one team, and the girls will be the other." She asked them to choose captains for their

3

teams. The boys chose Paul. The girls
chose Emily Asher.

"Mrs. Bernthal, what's the prize?" asked
Vanessa Nicolini.

"The prize?" repeated Mrs. Bernthal,
looking a bit surprised. "Oh, that's true.
Contests always have prizes, don't they?"

"Yes! Yes!" said the children.

She stopped for a moment to think. Robert wished they could just have a big party at the end. Then nobody would have to be a winner or a loser. Winning was fun, but losing a contest could make you feel awful. And Susanne Lee Rodgers, the smartest kid in the class, was a girl.

"The team that wins gets to throw a class party," said Mrs. Bernthal.

Robert almost fell off his chair. That was just what he was wishing for!

"The winners can choose their own decorations, music, party games, and treats," Mrs. Bernthal said. "Whatever you like."

The class clapped and shouted, "Hurray! We're having a party!" Lester Willis whistled. Mrs. Bernthal tried to frown at him, but she was still smiling.

Robert sat at his desk, frozen in place. Wow! Wait until Paul heard about this. He made a wish and it came true!

Getting Spooky

Paul frowned when Robert told him about getting his wish. "That's weird," he said.

"I know." Robert took the salami out of his sandwich and ate it. Then he ate the cheese and threw the bread away.

"We could use a little magic to win this contest," said Andy Liskin. They were all sitting at the same lunch table. "The girls have Susanne Lee on their team."

"I have all the books in the *Weird & Wacky Facts* series except for #23," said

Robert. "You can all borrow them. If we memorize the facts, maybe the boys can beat the girls."

The boys looked doubtful, but agreed to try.

After lunch, Robert sat down at his table and took out his math book with the brown cover. They always did math when they got back from lunch.

"I wish we could just skip math for once," he whispered across the table to Paul. Paul smiled in agreement.

Mrs. Bernthal took out a book with a shiny blue cover. It was not their math book. Robert looked at Paul. Paul stared back at Robert. "You're really getting spooky!" he whispered. Robert swallowed hard.

Mrs. Bernthal opened the book. "This poem is called 'Thief.' It's by Audrey B. Baird." She read:

Like the Sandman,
Storm Man
slips through the night,
a bag of rain
on his shoulder.
Wind gusts
from his nostrils!
Lightning flashes
from his fingers!
Thunder crashes
when he opens his bag!

And, like a thief,
Storm Man steals slumber away.

Robert could not believe it. As Mrs. Bernthal talked, explaining how the author wrote a poem to express her feelings about a storm, Robert looked at Paul. Paul's eyes were bugging out. He whispered, "Wish for no homework." Then he laughed.

Robert laughed, too. It *was* kind of funny. Twice in one day, he'd gotten what he wished for. He had never been this lucky before.

For the rest of the afternoon, the class wrote poems. Robert's poem was about Sally, the class snake.

Guess Who It Is?
by Robert Dorfman

There is a girl in my class I like a lot.
Melissa, Kristi, and
Susanne Lee it's not.

She is the best girl in school.
She is really, really cool.

She doesn't giggle or
talk all the time.
She never, never feels like slime!

Here is a clue.
  She is like a worm, only longer.
    Like a hose, only shorter.
        I like her best when
            she makes her S.

      Did you guess?

    Yes!

  I'm in charge of Sally the Snake.
I even feed her when she is awake.

  Everyone would like this job, I bet.
        Because Sally Snake is
            a great class pet.

Robert liked the way the words wiggled on the page like Sally did.

On the way home, he and Paul talked about the contest.

"We're going to have to work extra hard to win this contest," said Paul.

"I know," said Robert. "It's going to be hard to beat the girls. Susanne Lee knows everything!"

"At least you and I have read all the *Weird & Wacky Facts* books," said Paul.

"If the rest of the boys read them, maybe we can win," said Robert.

"Remember to bring some in on Monday," Paul said.

"Okay. If only Susanne Lee wasn't in the contest," said Robert, "we would at least have a chance."

Paul nodded in agreement. They walked the rest of the way home without saying anything.

Special Powers

On Monday, Susanne Lee was out sick.

"Uh-oh," said Paul. "Your wish came true."

"What wish?"

"On Friday, you said if only Susanne Lee wasn't in the contest, the boys would have a better chance at winning."

"That wasn't a wish," said Robert. Or was it? He didn't wish for her to be sick. Was it the same thing?

Paul smiled and shrugged. "Just joking," he said.

Robert knew he was having some weird luck lately. First he wished for a class party, and he got his wish. Then he wished they could skip math, and they did. And now maybe he got another wish, even if he didn't mean for it to be one.

"She's probably got swollen tonsils or something," said Paul, trying to comfort Robert. Paul knew about that because he was out a few weeks ago when his tonsils were swollen. "She'll probably be back in class tomorrow."

Robert sure hoped so. This was making him nervous. It was like he had special powers or something.

He couldn't stop worrying the whole rest of the day. He worried all through dinner and that evening, too. He phoned Paul.

"What if I do have the power to make someone sick?" he said.

"Why? Did another wish come true?"

Paul was beginning to sound really interested.

"No, but I'm afraid to open my mouth," said Robert.

"You can't keep your mouth closed forever," said Paul. "Just don't make any more

wishes. Promise. Cross your heart and say, 'I will not make another wish.'"

Robert thought that was good advice. With his hand over his heart, he said, "I will not make another wish. I promise."

Jail

Susanne Lee was out sick the next day, too. Mrs. Bernthal said Susanne Lee's mother had called. Susanne Lee had a very bad cold and might be out for several days. "It would be nice if you all made get-well cards. I will see that they are delivered to her," said Mrs. Bernthal.

Several days. How many was that? Three? Four? Could she still be out on Monday, the day of the contest?

Robert took a piece of yellow construction paper. Yellow was a good color for a

get-well card. It was like sunshine. Robert wished he could feel as cheerful as the yellow paper. He felt gray. The color of a cement block. Cement blocks reminded him of jail.

He wondered if he could go to jail for making Susanne Lee sick. He'd be the youngest person there, probably.

Paul was hunched over his get-well card. It was orange. There was a rainbow on it and a spaceship. Paul always drew spaceships. He was a good artist. Robert had one of Paul's spaceship drawings on the wall of his room. Paul had almost thrown it out, but Robert had rescued it.

"Some ten-year-olds have gone to prison," he told Paul.

"Really?" Paul looked up from his drawing.

"Yes," said Robert. "I saw it once on television." Paul thought about that for a second, then went back to his drawing.

"If I go to prison, I might not see my mom or dad—or even Charlie—for a long time. And Mrs. Bernthal would probably forget me."

"You won't go to prison," said Paul.

"How do you know?"

"You're only eight. You were never in prison before. You never did anything illegal. I

19

don't think they can put you in jail unless you have a record."

"What kind of record?"

"It's like a report that shows if you did a crime before." Paul was rubbing some eraser dust off his paper and deciding which color to use next.

Robert wondered about the time in the park when he dropped a candy wrapper on the sidewalk by mistake. He thought he had tossed it into the wastebasket, but it must have bounced off the edge of the basket and landed on the ground. A park attendant saw it and yelled at him for littering and asked him his name. Robert told him. Could the attendant have reported Robert to the police? Could you go to jail for littering?

"Well, what if I do go to prison? I could grow old in jail. Maybe my mom would come visit me with chocolate-covered jelly cookies. But it would only be for a few minutes,

and we would have to talk through a glass window, on telephones. I saw that on TV. Would you write me letters?"

"What? Oh, sure." Paul was startled out of his concentration.

"What will happen to Fuzzy and Flo and Billie?" Robert had a pet-sitting service, and his tarantula, Fuzzy, and the doves, Flo and Billie, had been given to him by people who couldn't take care of them anymore. He had promised he would take good care of them.

"Stop thinking like that," said Paul. "You're being gloomy. You are not going to jail. Just don't make any more wishes."

"Well, okay, but if I did go to jail, would you take care of Fuzzy and Flo and Billie?"

"Sure," said Paul.

Paul was a good friend. Robert felt better.

Robert folded the yellow construction paper and took out green and orange

markers. Inside the card, he drew a bird singing. He even drew in a music note near the bird so you would know it was singing. He wasn't sure if the little round part on the note went in front of the line, like a *d*, or behind it, like a *b*. He made it like a *b* and colored it in. He wrote:

TO SUSANNE LEE,
FROM ROBERT D.,
I'M SORRY YOUR SICK,
GET WELL QUICK.

As Mrs. Bernthal walked around the room, she saw Robert's card and corrected it to read:

TO SUSANNE LEE,
FROM ROBERT D.,
I'M SORRY YOU'RE SICK,
GET WELL QUICK.

"Very nice, Robert," she said.

Robert drew a picture of a box of tissues on the front. He remembered how important tissues were when he had a cold. Still, something was missing.

"Take your cards home to finish them," said Mrs. Bernthal. Robert put his inside his loose-leaf notebook to take it home with him.

Breaking the Spell

Robert's mom was making a cup of tea in the kitchen when he got home.

"Hello, Rob," she said. "Did you have a good day?"

"Uh-huh," he said, putting down his book bag and unzipping it. He took out the card he had made for Susanne Lee and showed it to his mom.

"That's very nice, Rob," she said. "I like the box of tissues."

"Thanks," Robert said. His mom could always see what he was trying to draw.

Melissa Thurm had looked at his card in school and asked him why he'd drawn an iceberg on his get-well card.

He opened the kitchen drawer, where his mom kept a box of cough drops. He

took out three cough drops and wrapped them in a piece of aluminum foil.

"What are those for?" asked his mom.

"They're for Susanne Lee. She has a cold."

"Oh," said his mom.

Upstairs, in his room, he taped the foil package to the card. Then he took a tissue from the box near his bed and cut a little square out of it and glued one end of it to the box of tissues. It looked like a tissue was popping out of the top of the box.

Now the card was ready to send. He put it back in his book bag to take to school tomorrow.

Robert lay in bed staring at the ceiling. He thought about people in stories who were granted wishes. Sometimes things turned out all right, like in "Thumbelina" when the old woman wanted a child and got her wish. But there were other times when wishes backfired, like in "The Fisherman and His Wife," when the fisherman's wife got too greedy and asked for more and more until finally everything was taken away and she was back where she started, with nothing.

Robert got up and turned on the light. He took out his book of fairy tales. Let's see. To break a spell, you had to kiss a frog. No. You had to be a princess for that

one. Another story said you had to slay a dragon! No way. There were no dragons in River Edge, New Jersey. He turned out the light and went back to bed.

As he lay there, Robert remembered *The Wizard of Oz*. He had just seen the movie on TV for the second time. Dorothy had to get the broom from the Wicked Witch of the West to go back to Kansas. Robert didn't see how he could do anything like that.

Then Robert thought of something else. The people in the fairy tales got three wishes, max. They never got more than three. Maybe that was the limit on wishes. Robert had had three wishes. He used one wish on the party. He used another wishing the class would skip math. And he used the third—he took a deep breath—on wishing Susanne Lee would not be in the contest.

And now it looked like that one was coming true! Maybe his powers were all used up!

The only way to know, of course, was to make another wish. But he'd promised he wouldn't. He had to talk to Paul.

One More Wish

"I have to make one more wish," said Robert.

"You promised!"

"I know. But the only way I can tell if the spell is broken is to make another wish. If it doesn't come true, then we'll know everything is back to normal. Nobody ever has more than three wishes in stories. Maybe I don't have to worry anymore!"

"Hmmm," said Paul. "Okay. But you have to be very careful. Don't do anything yet. After school, I'll come over to your house."

"Great." Robert couldn't wait.

The day seemed to crawl by, but finally the bell rang. Paul walked home with Robert and called his mother from there. "I'm over at Robert's," he said.

The boys sat together in Robert's beanbag chair, where they did their best thinking.

"What should I wish for?" asked Robert.

"You can wish for the phone to ring," Paul suggested.

"It might be someone we don't want to talk to," said Robert.

"Good point." Paul settled down to think again.

"I think we need a snack first," said Robert. His stomach had growled twice already.

"Hey! I have an idea!" said Paul.

"What is it?" asked Robert.

"You know how your mom never has good kid food in the refrigerator?"

"Yeah." Robert's mom kept cookies in the cupboard, and sometimes chips, but the stuff in the refrigerator was usually gross, grown-up food. And sometimes the milk was not too fresh because she forgot to buy a new container before the old one went bad.

"Okay. Let's wish for great food, then."

Robert liked that idea. He was starving. "Blueberry pie," he said. The last time he was at Paul's house, Mrs. Felcher had given them blueberry pie that she made herself.

"Brownies," said Paul, licking his lips.

"Chocolate milk," added Robert.

"Marshmallow-fudge, chocolate-chip, peanut-butter ice cream," said Paul.

"Pizza!"

"Cupcakes!"

Their mouths were watering as they thumped down the stairs.

Robert opened the refrigerator door. They found a bunch of carrots and a container of yogurt and something in a clear wrapper that could be bread.

After a moment, Robert shouted, "Hurray!" and spun around. Paul was there, ready for a high five.

"Congratulations!" Paul said. "The spell is broken!"

Robert took some cookies down from the cupboard. "In a way, I'm sorry," he said.

"Why? Did you want blueberry pie that badly?"

"No, it's not that," said Robert. "I figured if I still had wishes, I could wish for Susanne Lee not to be sick."

"Yeah," said Paul.

Quietly, the boys went upstairs to do their homework.

"The Person I Admire"

Robert had to admit, he felt a little sad not having his special powers anymore. The contest was coming up on Monday. The boys were all reading *Weird & Wacky Facts* books, hoping to get an edge. But nobody knew yet whether Susanne Lee would be back in time to be on the girls' team. It was tempting to think about making a wish to win.

"Susanne Lee thanked you for all the cards and poems you sent her," said Mrs.

Bernthal. "She said they really cheered her up. She has them taped to her bedroom wall so she can see them and think of you. She misses you and being here and hopes to be back with you soon."

Paul gathered the boys together at recess. "Don't worry," he told them. "We're okay, whether Susanne Lee comes back in time for the contest or not. Keep reading. I'm sure we can win."

At lunch, the boys spouted facts to one another.

"An armadillo always has four babies at a time, all girls or all boys," said Brian Hoberman.

Matt Blakey jumped in with the fact that people once believed that horseradish was a cure for headaches.

"Hi, boys," said Emily. "Are you ready for the contest?"

"Emily!" cried Joey. The boys snapped

to attention. "Um, yeah, we're ready. How about you?"

"We're in good shape," said Emily. "Good luck. May the best team win." She left, carrying a big load of books in her arms. She was probably memorizing all kinds of facts, too.

After math, Mrs. Bernthal told the class to get out their notebooks and write about someone they admired. "It could be a famous person, like a president, or an inventor, or an explorer."

"What about Martin Luther King, Jr.?" asked Emily Asher.

"Martin Luther King, Jr., is fine," said Mrs. Bernthal.

"Can I do Frankenstein?" Lester Willis shouted out.

"Frankenstein is the name of the doctor who created the monster. Is that who you mean?"

"No," said Lester. "I want to write about the monster."

"You admire the monster?"

"Yeah. He's cool." Lester Willis looked truly happy with his idea.

"Well, yes, I guess so, then," said Mrs. Bernthal. "You can also write about one of your parents or grandparents, or an uncle or aunt you especially admire."

"How about a teacher?" asked Vanessa Nicolini.

"Why, yes," said Mrs. Bernthal, blushing. "A teacher would be fine."

Robert wrote about Susanne Lee Rodgers. He wrote:

I ADMIRE SUSANNE LEE RODGERS BECAUSE SHE IS VERY SMART.

Robert thought about how she had helped him when he was in the lowest reading group. When she said, "That's very good, Robert," it made him grind his teeth, but she did help him move up to a higher reading group.

He wrote:

I ADMIRE HER FOR GETTING 100 ON ALL HER SPELLING TESTS.

Actually, she got 100 on *all* her tests, except one time when she got one math problem wrong and nearly cried.

He wrote:

I ADMIRE HER BECAUSE SHE HAS A WATCH THAT CAN TELL WHAT TIME IT IS ALL OVER THE WORLD.

Finally, he wrote:

I ADMIRE SUSANNE LEE BECAUSE SHE SAID NICE THINGS TO US EVEN THOUGH SHE WAS SICK.

Then he added in a hurry:

I'M SORRY SUSANNE LEE IS SICK AND IT'S MY FAULT. I HAVE THESE SPECIAL POWERS AND WISHED SOMETHING TERIBLE. IT WAS AN ACSIDENT. I DIDN'T EVEN NO I HAD THEM UNTIL IT WAS TO LATE.

There. He'd said it. Robert wondered how he could make it up to Susanne Lee. He realized he was grinding his teeth.

The Secret Is Out

As Robert took his seat the next morning, he sensed there was something new in the classroom. The essays they'd written yesterday were graded, and some were hanging on the bulletin boards around the room.

Robert's eyes stopped on his own essay, tacked up on the bulletin board on the coat closet door. It had a red B+ on it. That was the first time ever that he'd gotten more than a B in Mrs. Bernthal's class.

As they put away their jackets and book bags, the children read some of the essays.

"Hey, Robert," said Matt. "Can you make me fly?"

"Um, the spell is over," Robert answered.

"That's too bad," said Kristi Mills. "I thought you could make it be summer vacation."

"Well, um, I'm sorry." Robert felt a bit like he was the toothpaste in a tube that was being squeezed.

"Don't worry about it, Robert," said Paul. "They'll get over it."

"Class," said Mrs. Bernthal, clapping for everyone's attention. "Your contest will be on Monday. You have all weekend to get ready. Be sure to put on your thinking caps before you leave your house on Monday morning."

Mrs. Bernthal always talked like that. She told them they had to wear their thinking caps, and even drew one on the board with a lightbulb on it. "The lightbulb," she said, "is to show that the person wearing the cap is thinking."

Paul reminded the boys during recess what their team's strategy would be. "Think before shouting out an answer," he said. Paul looked right at Lester when he said it.

"Okay," said Lester, grinning.

Paul continued, "If you aren't sure what the question is, ask Mrs. Bernthal to repeat it." The boys nodded.

Finally, Paul said, "Don't listen to what the girls say. They will try to make us nervous, but it's just to scare us."

"And we're doing a good job of it, too," said Abby Ranko, startling them. The boys spun around.

"A spy!" said Joey.

Abby laughed again and walked away.

"I wish Robert still had his powers," said Matt.

"Me, too!" said Kevin Kransky.

Me, too, Robert thought.

Pep Talk

Robert's stomach did a flip-flop when he walked into the classroom on Monday morning. Susanne Lee was back. It was great to see she was all right, but it meant the boys would lose the contest now.

"Robert, can't you try your powers, just in case?" asked Joey.

Robert explained, "Even if I still had my powers, which I don't, I wouldn't use them. They can get people into trouble."

"Yeah," said Matt, "but we need help to win the contest."

Robert didn't argue with Matt. It was no use. Everyone thought having special powers was such fun.

"Hey, guys," said Paul, jumping in, "you memorized all those facts in the *Weird & Wacky Facts* books. Maybe we'll win. And if we win, we'll have a great party with gummy worms, and vampire teeth, and

those cans of green slime we can spray on one another." Robert admired Paul for giving the boys a good pep talk.

"Yeah!" said Lester.

"Ee-yew!" said Susanne Lee, coming up behind them. "That stuff is gross!"

"Hey, Susanne Lee. How are you feeling?" asked Andy.

"I'm fine, thank you," said Susanne Lee.

"Hi," said Robert. "I—I'm glad you're better."

"Thanks, Robert," said Susanne Lee. She looked at Matt. "It's important to work hard for what you want. Then you'll know you earned it."

Robert almost felt his teeth grinding. Then he remembered how glad he was that Susanne Lee was not sick anymore, and he felt better.

"Are we ready to begin?" asked Mrs. Bernthal.

"YES!" said the class all at once.

"Okay, then," said Mrs. Bernthal. "Let's begin!"

"It's now or never," whispered Paul. Robert tried to smile.

The Best Party

"There are nine boys and eleven girls," said Mrs. Bernthal. "Boys, you line up over here on this side of the room." She pointed to her left. The boys scrambled for places against the chalkboard wall.

"And girls over there," said Mrs. Bernthal, pointing to the opposite side. The girls went to their places, against the supply cabinets.

"I will give each side a question," said Mrs. Bernthal, holding a sheet of paper. "You may talk over your answer with

your teammates, if you wish. If your final answer is correct, your team will get one point. After each side has answered twenty questions, we'll count up the points. The team with the most points is the winner of the contest."

The children were buzzing with talk, eager to begin. They got quiet as Mrs. Bernthal read the first question to the boys.

"Which President of the United States weighed more than three hundred pounds?"

Paul, as captain of the boys' team, was first. He turned to the other boys and whispered. "I think I know it!" he said. Andy nodded. The others nodded, too.

"William Howard Taft," said Paul.

"That's correct," said Mrs. Bernthal. "One point for the boys."

The girls' first question went to Emily Asher.

"What is the largest island in the

world?" asked Mrs. Bernthal, moving to the next question.

Emily turned to Susanne Lee and the other girls. She wasn't sure. Susanne Lee whispered to her. Emily turned to Mrs. Bernthal and said, "Greenland."

"That is correct," said Mrs. Bernthal. She made a mark on her score sheet.

The questions went pretty quickly. The score was almost even for a while. Then the boys missed two in a row. The girls applauded whenever the boys got an answer wrong. Robert felt his confidence slipping, even though he had answered two questions correctly.

Paul tried to cheer the boys up with another pep talk. "Come on, guys, we can do it! Don't give up. We can't let the girls beat us."

The girls did win, in the end. The boys were good sports, though, even if they could not count on having green slime at the party.

Emily Asher made a victory statement, thanking the boys for a good contest. Then she invited them all to the girls' party tomorrow. She said she was sure they

would enjoy it, even if there were no vampire teeth. The boys groaned.

Susanne Lee got up to say her mother would make cupcakes for everyone, with pink frosting on them.

"What about gummy worms?" asked Lester.

"Oh, boys are so gross," said Melissa Thurm, walking away.

Robert and Paul looked at each other.

"Don't you wish you had another wish right now?" asked Paul.

"You bet!" said Robert, imagining Melissa Thurm finding a bag of real worms. "But I promised. No more wishes."

"Right!" said Paul, giving Robert a high five.

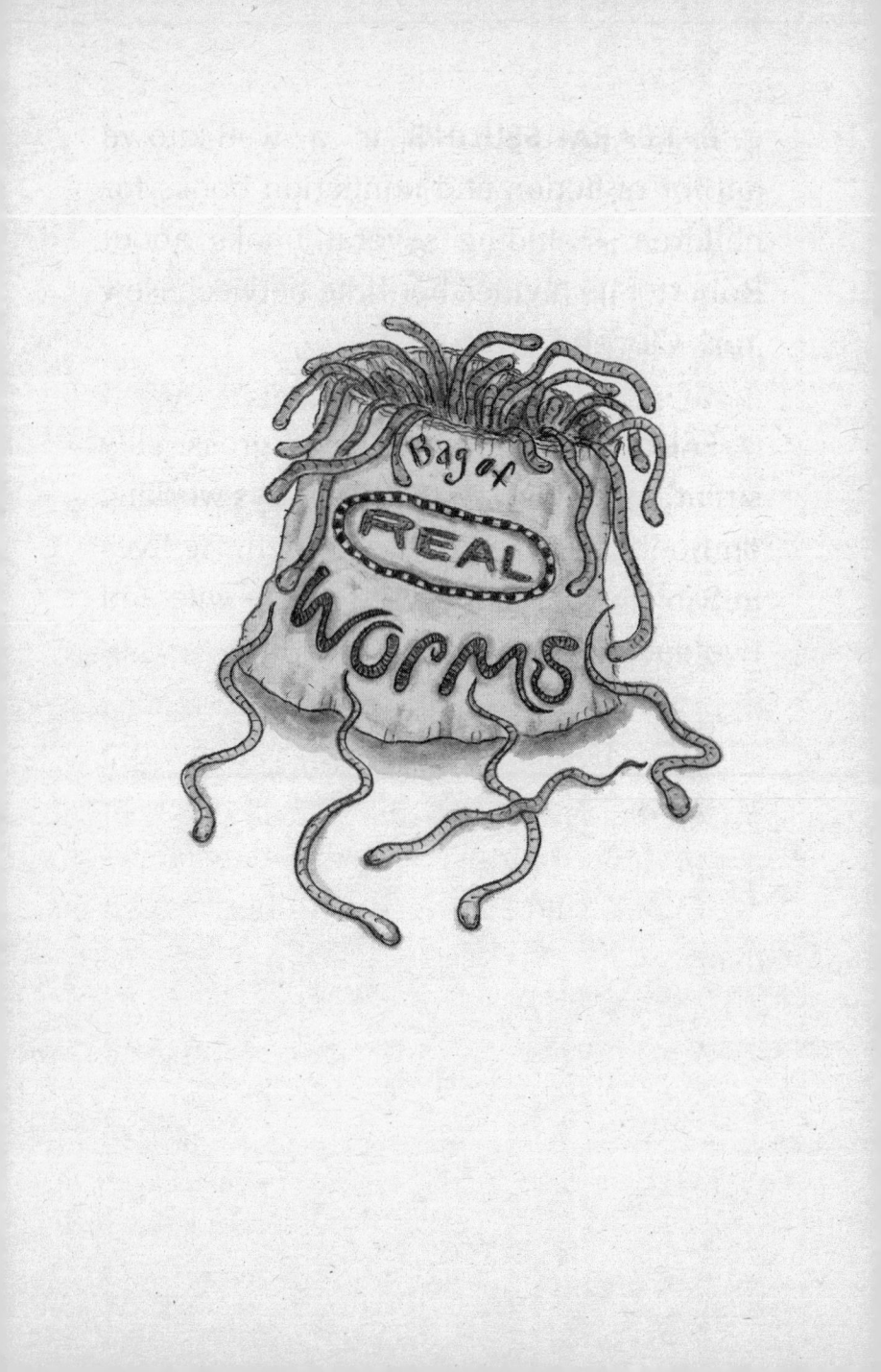

BARBARA SEULING is a well-known author of fiction and nonfiction books for children, including several books about Robert. She divides her time between New York City and Vermont.

PAUL BREWER likes to draw gross, silly situations, which is why he enjoys working on books about Robert so much. He lives in San Diego, California, with his wife and two daughters.